Abby Levine

You Push, I Ride

pictures by Margot Apple

Puffin Books

PUFFIN BOOKS
Published by the Penguin Group
Viking Penguin, a division of Penguin Books USA Inc.,
375 Hudson Street, New York, New York 10014, U.S.A.
Penguin Books Ltd, 27 Wrights Lane, London W8 5TZ, England
Penguin Books Australia Ltd, Ringwood, Victoria, Australia
Penguin Books Canada Ltd, 2801 John Street, Markham, Ontario, Canada L3R 1B4
Penguin Books (N.Z.) Ltd, 182–190 Wairau Road, Auckland 10, New Zealand

Penguin Books Ltd, Registered Offices: Harmondsworth, Middlesex, England

First published in the United States of America by Albert Whitman & Company, 1989
Published in Picture Puffins, 1990
1 3 5 7 9 10 8 6 4 2
Text copyright © Abby Levine, 1989
Illustrations copyright © Margot Apple, 1989
All rights reserved

LIBRARY OF CONGRESS CATALOGING IN PUBLICATION DATA
Levine, Abby.   You push, I ride / by Abby Levine ;
illustrated by Margot Apple.   p.   cm.—(Picture puffins)
Summary: Rhymed text and illustrations describe the activities of
a little pig's day.
ISBN 0-14-054180-2
[1. Pigs—Fiction.   2. Stories in rhyme.]   I. Apple, Margot, ill.
II. Title.
[PZ8.3.L576Yo   1990]   [E]—dc20   90-32481

Printed in the United States of America
Set in Helvetica

For Hanna, who does all jobs well. A.L.

For the Lawless family: Jane, Michael, Tyrone,
and most of all, Zachary. M.A.

I shake,
you wake.

I brush, you shave.

You leave,
I wave.

We clear away
and start our day.

You tie,
you snap,
you zip,
I wrap.

We go outside.
You push,
I ride.

We shop,
we walk.

I wait,
you talk.

I shout,
I sing,
I slide,
I swing.

You chat,
you watch,
you push,
you catch.

You make a lap.

I take a nap.

I build, I stack.

I put things back.

I say, "Who is it?"

when friends come to visit.

You cook,
I look.

I feed the cat.
(I can do that!)

I eat green things so I'll grow tall.

You eat, but you don't grow at all.

You fill the tub.
I sail, you scrub.

I drip,
you rub.

We hug, we kiss.
We all do this!

You say, "Good night"
and turn off the light.

I sleep tight.